A Running Press® Miniature Edition™
© 2013 by Running Press
Printed in China
TLF

9
Digit on the right indicates the number of this printing

Library of Congress Control Number: 2012952331

ISBN 978-0-7624-4869-2
Published by Running Press Book Publishers
An Imprint of Perseus Books, LLC.
A Subsidiary of Hachette Book Group, Inc.
2300 Chestnut Street
Philadelphia, PA 19103-4371

Visit us on the web!
www.runningpress.com

CONTENTS

INTRODUCTION

When we think of Sherlock Holmes, a picture usually pops immediately to mind: a man wearing a deerstalker cap, smoking a curved pipe, and uttering the well-known quip, "Elementary, my dear Watson." Interestingly, none of those traits are mentioned in Sir Arthur Conan Doyle's novels and short stories. But it hardly matters.

Sherlock Holmes is so ingrained in our imaginations and our culture, it is difficult to think of the world without him. Ever since Doyle first brought Holmes to life in 1887 with the publication of *A Study in Scarlet*, there have been scores of illustrations, plays, movies, TV adaptations, and spin-off novels inspired by this curious character.

There's just something about Sherlock Holmes: most notably, his remarkable powers of observation and logical reasoning. He is eccentric, to be sure, but he uses his singular talents for good by solving crime. He has a mind like a steel trap, but as noted in the first novel, his "ignorance [is] as great as his knowledge." He knows little of literature or philosophy. On the other hand, he can recall anything related to chemistry and is well-versed in narrow branches of science, all of which help him with his investigations. He has a strong sense of justice, but occasionally extends forgiveness to some of the culprits he corners. He is an excellent boxer and swordsman, and knows martial arts. And he's not a snob; he's as willing to go undercover in an opium den as he is to handle a case for a king.

Holmes' less admirable qualities, perhaps, are that he dabbles in a drug habit, has no interest in romantic love, and often seems to have no time for the "small talk" that is a normal part of everyday social exchanges. He remarks "I cannot live without brainwork," and when he doesn't have a crime to solve he often mopes around his flat at 221b Baker Street, making up a "7 percent solution" of cocaine, or morosely playing his violin.

Though human relationships are

not his strength, he displays keen insight into human nature. He is also a talented mimic, able to fool people with his crafty disguises. And of course, he has a capacity for friendship, as shown by his alliance with his most trusted sidekick, Dr. John Watson.

The character of Dr. Watson provides a frame for the mysteries. Most of the novels and short stories read like Watson's journal, where he dutifully reports the details of all the cases he has witnessed. Watson serves as a narrator, as Holmes' accomplice in the investigations, as well as a foil helping showcase Holmes' gifts for deduction.

The mysteries usually follow a formula: Someone calls upon Holmes to solve a case. The police are sometimes involved, but sometimes not. There is often an exciting scene involving a sting, chase, or an attack. At the end, Holmes explains the logical reasoning that led him to the villain. The conceit is satisfying—though in some cases, Holmes is not successful. But that just helps to make him more human.

Indeed, Sherlock Holmes seems more "human" and "real" than perhaps any other character in literature. Scholars have endeavored to construct biographies of Holmes, speculating on his year of birth, for example, or whether he attended Cambridge or Oxford. When he "died," fans wore black armbands. It is ironic that a character known for his cold and calculating reason should inspire such passionate devotion. Perhaps if we asked Holmes to account for his more-than-a-century-long popularity, he might take a draw on his pipe and simply reply, "Elementary."

THE "LIFE" OF SHERLOCK HOLMES

SHERLOCK HOLMES WAS "BORN" with Sir Arthur Conan Doyle's first novel, *A Study in Scarlet*, which ran in *Beeton's Christmas Annual* in 1887. The story is set a few years before, in 1881, and begins with Watson just returning from the war in Afghanistan and seeking a flatmate. Watson and Holmes meet and take rooms at 221b Baker Street. Holmes already has a thriving business as a "consulting detective," and soon he enlists Watson's help with his investigations. The first mystery has the duo assisting Scotland Yard in cracking a case.

The second Holmes novel, *The Sign of Four*, was published serially in *Lippincott's* magazine in 1890. In it, a young woman consults Holmes on her father's disappearance. That woman eventually becomes Watson's wife, inciting Watson to leave his bachelor quarters at Baker Street.

Due to the popularity of the novels, Doyle was persuaded to have Holmes and Watson continue their adventures. Doyle then insisted on writing short stories, as he thought it would be more satisfying for readers to experience a mystery in one sitting, rather than wait for the next installment. He wrote six stories, which all ran in *The Strand Magazine*. They were accompanied by the illustrations of Sidney Paget, who depicted Holmes with the now-famous deerstalker hat and traveling cape. This group of stories was then published as *The Adventures of Sherlock Holmes* (1891). In them, Watson and Holmes no longer share rooms, but

Dr. Watson frequently comes to call at Baker Street.

The Strand Magazine, and the thousands of Holmes fans, were now clamoring for more stories. But by that time, Doyle was growing tired of his creation. He had always felt that Holmes had taken him away from his more serious writing pursuits. Doyle told his mother he was thinking of killing off his hero, and she dissuaded him, giving him a plot idea for what would later become "The Adventure of the Copper Beeches." He wrote several more stories for *The Strand* (compiled in *The Memoirs of Sherlock Holmes* in 1893). In the last of this collection ("The Final Problem"), Doyle finally took the plunge, as it were, by having Holmes fall to his death at Reischenbach Falls. The reading public was bereft.

Doyle eventually gave in to fan pressure to write another Holmes story, which resulted in the novel *The Hound of the Baskervilles* (1901). He does not resurrect his hero, but merely writes of a case that happened before Holmes' fateful tumble over the falls. *The Hound of the Baskervilles* is considered (by most fans, scholars, and Doyle himself) to be the best of the Sherlock Holmes tales, rich in atmosphere and symbolism.

But *The Hound of the Baskervilles* was not enough to satisfy his readers. In 1903 Doyle officially brought Holmes back to life and wrote another batch of stories, explaining that Holmes had not died at the falls, but had gone into hiding for a few years. These tales were published as *The Return of Sherlock Holmes* in 1905. A final novel, *The Valley of Fear*, appeared in 1915. The short story collection, *His Last Bow* (1917), had Holmes helping the government at the start of World War I, then having him retire to Sussex, where he immersed himself in his beekeeping hobby. Doyle never provided any details as to how his most famous sleuth finally met his end.

What follows in this little book are plot summaries of Sherlock

Holmes' "most essential mysteries." Surely there will be a reader who will be disappointed to find their particular favorite not included. Apologies in advance. Yet the determination of the choices comes largely from what Sherlock fans and Arthur Conan Doyle himself considered the best Holmes tales. All are designed to be enjoyed "in just one sitting." *But be forewarned: the mysteries are revealed!*

Ideally, these should be read on a cold, foggy day, so one can recreate the feeling of late Victorian London. But donning a deerstalker cap and smoking a pipe are definitely not required.

ESSENTIAL CHARACTERS IN THE WORLD OF SHERLOCK HOLMES

Dr. John Watson: Former army surgeon who finds himself accomplice and witness to Holmes' brilliant methods of deduction.

Inspector Lestrade: A Scotland Yard official who is often stumped with cases, and calls on Holmes for help.

The Baker Street Irregulars: A band of street urchins who do much of Holmes' legwork in his investigations.

Mrs. Hudson: Holmes' landlady at 221b Baker Street, she lives downstairs and provides a hot meal and common sense when needed.

Irene Adler: The only woman to outsmart Holmes—and perhaps the only one to captivate him.

Professor Moriarty: Holmes' arch-nemesis and mastermind of many of the evil schemes in London and beyond.

Mycroft Holmes: Sherlock's older brother, seven years his senior, who works as a government agent. He does not appear until the later stories (the first being "The Adventure of the Greek Interpreter"), which are not included in this mini-tome.

A STUDY IN SCARLET

"There is a scarlet thread of murder running through the colourless skein of life, and our duty is to unravel it, isolate it, and expose every inch of it."
—Sherlock Holmes

D R. WATSON, AN ARMY surgeon, has been wounded in the Second

Anglo-Afghan war, and has come to London for a long recuperation. A bachelor without any relations, he needs someone to help share costs for lodgings. A friend leads him to Sherlock Holmes, and the two settle on comfortable rooms at No. 221b Baker Street.

Watson finds his new flatmate generally agreeable, but a very curious study. First, his areas of expertise are decidedly narrow.

Holmes knows nothing of the Solar System, but he has a profound knowledge of chemistry, especially about poisons. Holmes remarks to Watson that a man's brain is "like a little empty attic, and you have to stock it with such furniture as you choose.... It is of the highest importance, therefore, not to have useless facts elbowing out the useful ones."

Watson notices that Holmes gets

a steady stream of callers, which Holmes calls "clients." Eventually, Holmes reveals that he has a "turn for observation and deduction" and he makes a living by solving crimes and other mysterious events that require an explanation. Watson gets his first taste of what this means when a letter is delivered from Scotland Yard asking Holmes to come to a crime scene. Holmes tells Watson to get his hat, and thus starts Watson's adventures...

A body has been found in an empty house on Brixton Road. The identification in the victim's pockets indicates that he is one Enoch J. Drebber, of Cleveland, Ohio. There was also a letter addressed to someone by the name of Joseph Stangerson. No marks of violence were found on the victim, but there was some blood in the room.

When Holmes and Watson arrive, they are met by Inspectors Gregson and Lestrade. Holmes sniffs the dead man's lips; then as the body is moved, a woman's wedding ring falls to the floor. Holmes lights a match and finds that the word "Rache" has been written in blood on the wall. Gregson immediately assumes the crime has to do with someone named "Rachel." Holmes continues his strange methods of investigation, carefully making calculations with his tape measure and looking at surfaces through a large magnifying glass.

Finally, he proclaims he may have something that might help the Inspectors: The murderer is a tall man with small feet, who wears square-toed boots and smokes a certain kind of cigar. He also says that the victim died of poisoning, and that "Rache" is German for "revenge."

They interview the constable who found the body, and he states that there had been a drunk man hanging about the gate at the time he made his discovery. A harmless enough person, he says. A frustrated Holmes tells him plainly that the "drunk" was in fact the murderer, playing at intoxication to make an easy escape. Holmes figures the murderer must have come back for the ring, but was stymied by the constable's appearance.

Holmes puts an ad in the paper to advertise that a lost ring has been found near Brixton Road. It's a trap that he hopes will bring the murderer directly to him. An old woman comes to claim the ring, saying that it belongs to her daughter. After she leaves, Holmes runs to follow her trail, trusting she will lead him to the culprit. Alas, Holmes realizes the old woman was actually a young man in disguise, who has cleverly shaken Holmes' pursuit.

The next day, Watson is introduced to what Holmes calls, "the Baker Street division of the detective police force," a group of urchins who work for Holmes. Later, Gregson visits Baker Street to smugly say he has found the murderer. Drebber had been staying at a boarding house, and had reportedly made advances to the proprietor's daughter. Gregson reasons that the culprit must be the brother of the compromised girl, who killed Drebber in a fit of rage. But Lestrade arrives with news that pokes a hole in Gregson's theory: Joseph Strangerson has been found in a hotel room, stabbed in the heart. Above him was the word "Rache" written in blood. The only clues found near the body are a telegram that reads "J.H. is in Europe," and a small case containing two pills.

Holmes states that those pills are the last piece of the puzzle. But first he must test his theory: He asks for his landlady's sick old terrier. He feeds one pill to the dog and it has no effect. Then he tries the other pill and the dog keels over dead. Holmes, now at peace, says he knows the identity of the murderer.

Gregson and Lestrade press Holmes to say more. Just then, one of Holmes' urchins knocks on the door to say a cab is waiting. Watson is puzzled, as Holmes seems like he is going on a sudden journey, and wonders what it could mean. Holmes asks the cabbie to help him with the buckle of his luggage, when suddenly there is a clicking sound; Holmes has handcuffed the cab driver. Holmes triumphantly presents Mr. Jefferson Hope, the murderer of Drebber and Stangerson!

✦✦✦

The novel suddenly shifts to flash back to a story that happened in another time and place: the Utah desert almost forty years before, in 1847. John Ferrier and a five-year-old girl named Lucy are the only survivors in a band of pioneers. Dying of hunger and thirst, they stumble upon a group of Mormons. The Mormons offer Ferrier and his charge safe refuge on the condition they adopt their religion. Ferrier agrees, but privately knows he will not accept their beliefs. The years pass, and Ferrier becomes a rich farmer, settling near Salt Lake City. He adopts the orphan Lucy, who grows to be quite a beauty. Lucy falls deeply in love with another pioneer named Jefferson Hope, and soon the two become engaged, with Ferrier's blessing.

But the Mormon elders forbid Lucy to marry a "gentile," someone not of the "true faith." They tell Ferrier that his daughter has a choice of marrying two prominent men in the Church: either Drebber or Strangerson. Ferrier argues that Hope is a good man, more than worthy of Lucy's hand. But the Mormons stand firm and Ferrier knows they will make good with their threats. He and Lucy have no choice but to flee their home, with Hope's help. It is a harrowing escape—a path made under cloak of night, through ravines and other perils of the Utah wilderness. Soon the Mormon elders are hot on their trail. Ferrier is shot dead by Stangerson, while Lucy is married off to Drebber. Within a month, Lucy dies of a broken heart. Hope vows to avenge their deaths, promising to follow Drebber and

Stangerson to the ends of the earth to take his revenge.

The novel shifts once again, forward to 1881 London, where Jefferson Hope explains to Holmes how he carried out the murders:

Mourning over Lucy's body before it was buried, Hope had removed Drebber's wedding ring from her finger. He carried that ring for twenty years, waiting for his chance at revenge. He wanted

Drebber to be staring at that ring the moment he died, so he would know exactly why his life was being taken. Over the course of two decades, Drebber became rich, while Stangerson worked as his secretary. The two had left the Mormon faith, leading lives of debauchery and hopping from town to town in America, eventually coming abroad to London. Hope's plan for revenge never wavered, and he followed them across the Atlantic. He got a job as a cabdriver, so that he could better follow them. Hope discovered he had a heart aneurysm, which threatened to take his life at any moment. Time became even more precious, and Hope finally got his chance one night.

A very drunk Drebber happened to hail Hope's cab. Hope drove him to an abandoned house. Once he led him through the door, Hope revealed his identity and gave Drebber the choice between two pills, declaring "Let the high God judge between us." Just when Drebber realized he chose the fatal pill, Hope held the ring before his eyes. Because of his heart affliction, Hope got a nosebleed right at that crucial moment. In a wave of mischief, he wrote the word "Rache" in his own blood on the wall, just to put the police off the scent. Soon he found Strangerson in a hotel room, and offered him the same choice. Strangerson attempted to attack Hope, who stabbed him in self-defense.

Hope goes on to explain a few loose ends to Holmes: He did indeed send a crafty friend to retrieve the ring, because he suspected a trap. Yet he didn't think another trap was being set when a street urchin told him that a cab was wanted at 221b Baker Street.

Soon after this confession, Hope dies. Inspectors Lestrade and Gregson get the public glory for solving the case. But Watson knows better. He has witnessed firsthand the extraordinary deductive powers of Sherlock Holmes and declares that he will record all the facts in his journal, so that others might eventually read of the great detective.

THE SIGN
OF FOUR

"When you have eliminated the impossible, whatever remains, however improbable, *must be the truth."*
— Sherlock Holmes

A YOUNG WOMAN NAMED Mary Morstan comes to call at Baker Street. She explains the background of her present quandary: Ten years before, her father, Captain Morstan, an officer in the Indian regiment, wrote to tell her he was coming home to England. But then he mysteriously disappeared. A few years later, she got a most extraordinary gift in the post: a single, lustrous pearl. Another pearl followed every year, and she now has a collection of six pearls, all worth a handsome sum.

Mary has just received an anonymous letter, summoning her to a clandestine meeting that evening, but assuring her, "If you are distrustful bring two friends. You are a wronged woman and shall have justice." It is signed "your unknown friend." She asks Holmes and Watson to accompany her, and the threesome make their way to the appointed place.

The "friend" turns out to be a peculiar man named Thaddeus Sholto, who divulges an incredible story: His father, Major John Sholto, was a close comrade of Mary's father in the army. He had returned from India a prosperous man. But he had a strange phobia of men with wooden legs. On his deathbed, he confessed to Thaddeus and his twin brother Bartholomew that he had wronged "poor Morstan's orphan." He went on to recount that he and Captain Morstan had come into possession of a great treasure while in India. Sholto had brought it over, and Morstan later returned to England to claim his share. The two old friends quarreled bitterly about its division, and Morstan became so heated during the argument that he keeled over from a heart attack. Worried that he would be blamed for Morstan's death, Sholto disposed of the body. He continues the account by revealing that his sin was not just in concealing his death, but in hiding the treasure and in denying Sholto's daughter her rightful inheritance. He was about to reveal the location of the treasure when suddenly he looked at the window and cried, "Keep him out!" Thaddeus and Bartholemew spotted a malevolent-looking man staring at them, but just as soon he was gone. Sholto died instantly from fright. The secret visitor left only a piece of paper that was signed, "The sign of the four."

In a gesture to make good for his father's wrong, Thaddeus had sent Mary a single pearl for the last six years. Without finding the treasure, there wasn't much else he could do. But then the most extraordinary thing happened: his brother Bartholomew at last found the treasure at his father's old house, Pondicherry Lodge! It's estimated to be worth more than a half million sterling. Thaddeus' plan is that he and Mary should go to the lodge that very night to claim their fair share.

When they arrive, they find the treasure gone and Bartholomew dead, killed by a poisonous thorn. Beside the body is a note reading,

"The sign of the four."

The police arrive on the scene, along with Inspector Athelney Jones. They mistakenly arrest Thaddeus for the crime. Holmes and Watson must investigate: not only to hunt down the treasure, but to find the real murderer.

Holmes gets a hound-dog to follow the scent of the perpetrators. From the clues, Holmes deduces that they are searching for a man named Jonathan Small, who has a wooden leg, along with his accomplice, who seems to be of diminutive stature. Their chase leads them to discover that Small and his companion have taken out a boat. Holmes enlists the help of the "Baker Street Irregulars," his gang of street urchins, to help get information at the wharf and lead them to the boat. Holmes disguises himself as an old seafarer and fools

Watson and Inspector Jones.

The search ends with a dramatic boat chase: Holmes and Watson fire their pistols, while Small's accomplice spews another poisonous thorn, narrowly missing them. The accomplice drowns, while Small is apprehended.

Jonathan Small tells his incredible story, which explains his motives:

He joined the English army in his

youth and was stationed in India. While swimming in the Ganges, a crocodile had taken his leg. After becoming a "peg leg," he got a job as an overseer on an Indian plantation. Then the Great Rebellion happened: Indians rose up against their white masters, and Small witnessed the massacre of the plantation's owners. To save his own skin, Small entered into a pact with three Indian men: he would help them kill a rich rajah and steal a treasure. They called their pact "The Sign of the Four," and took a solemn oath that they would stick together. The four were all eventually sentenced to life in prison for the murder, but were able to hide the treasure before their capture.

While at the penal colony, Small met Major Sholto and Colonel Morstan, who were overseeing the convicts. He made them a deal: if they could arrange for the four's escape, they could have a share of the treasure as well. Sholto and Morstan agreed, but Sholto outsmarted them all and fled to England with the entire treasure. Since then, Sholto had lived as a very wealthy man in England, but had a fear that Small would return for retribution.

Small did eventually get out of prison, and befriended an aboriginal from the Andaman Islands named Tonga. Together they traveled the world and eventually made it to England. Coincidentally, Small came to Sholto's house the night he died and had the satisfaction of seeing his foe die in terror, but he was no closer to getting his riches back. Years later, when he heard that Sholto's son had found the treasure, he came to claim it. He arrived at Pondicherry Lodge that night with the intention only to steal back the treasure, but Tonga, in a fit of savagery, killed Bartholomew. When Holmes and Watson were getting close on their trail, Small sprinkled the jewels in the ocean, saying that if he can't have the treasure, then no one can.

Though Mary loses her treasure, she gains another one: Watson proposes marriage to her at the end of the story, while Holmes, exhausted but satisfied with solving the case, languidly reaches for his cocaine bottle.

A SCANDAL IN BOHEMIA

"To Sherlock Holmes
she is always the *woman."*
—Dr. Watson

AN EXOTIC-LOOKING, MASK-wearing visitor pays a call to Holmes. His attempt to conceal his identity is in vain—Holmes already knows that he is the

King of Bohemia. The king confesses that he has come on a matter of utmost delicacy: He is about to be married to the Princess of Scandinavia, and a trinket from a former love affair could ruin his plans. Five years ago, he made the acquaintance of the opera singer and "well-known adventuress" Irene Adler. There is a photograph that proves their affair, and the King is tormented with the worry that Irene could send it to his betrothed. The King wants Holmes to retrieve that photograph at all costs.

Holmes stakes out Irene's house, Briony Lodge, disguised as an ill-kept groom. He observes she has one visitor, Godfrey Norton. Norton leaves the lodge and catches a cab. A few minutes later, Irene emerges and calls another cab, telling the driver to hurry to the church. Holmes follows in his disguise, where he unexpectedly witnesses their wedding. Holmes is not yet sure what to make of this surprising turn of events, but hopes now that Irene is married, she is less likely to publicize the compromising photo.

For his next visit to Briony Lodge, Holmes disguises himself as a clergyman and enlists Watson's help on the mission. He warns Watson that he must not interfere with any skirmish he might witness. Instead,

Holmes asks him to do something slightly illegal. Can he throw a smoke-rocket through Irene's window and yell "Fire!"? Watson agrees.

As Holmes and Watson approach the lodge they see Irene's carriage arriving at the doorstep. Suddenly a fight breaks out among men in the street, and Holmes (as a clergyman) steps in the middle of it, in order to protect the lady. A blow is struck, causing blood to stream down Holmes' face. He is taken inside the house to recover, while Watson throws the rocket. Chaos ensues. There's smoke, and some screams—but then assurances that it's all a false alarm.

Within ten minutes Holmes joins Watson on the street corner, grinning with satisfaction. Irene Adler has inadvertently shown him where the photograph is hidden. As they stroll back to Baker Street, he explains that everyone on the street was an accomplice to Holmes' plan, and the fight was carefully orchestrated as a way to get Holmes inside her house. Under the threat of fire, Irene had instinctively gone to protect her most prized possession, and now he knows that the photo is behind a secret sliding panel. Holmes plans to visit the house early the next morning with his client, so that the King might have the satisfaction of retrieving the photograph himself. After he concludes this report, they approach Holmes' doorstep. As he searches for the key, he hears a passer-by say "Good-night, Mr. Sherlock Holmes." It seems to have come from a youth wearing a heavy overcoat. He knows he has heard that voice before, he just can't place it . . .

The next morning, instead of finding the photograph, they find a letter addressed to Mr. Sherlock Holmes, saying, "You really did it very well. You took me in completely." In her note, Irene admits that she had been duped the night before—but quickly realized her mistake in revealing the photograph's hiding place. She compliments Holmes on his clergyman disguise, but reveals that she is also rather good at disguises: She was the young man who had followed him to his door and wished him a good night. By the time Holmes reads this letter, she writes, she and Norton will have already made their get-away. She will keep the photograph, but the King can rest assured that it will not be made public. In its place, she encloses her portrait, saying that the King may have it as a memento of their time together.

The King is jubilant at the news, saying that the cunning Irene would have made an "admirable queen" but regrets she wasn't of his station. Holmes makes a quick but cold comeback, noting that the lady is indeed "on a very different level to your Majesty." The King asks what he can do to thank Holmes for saving his reputation. He offers a precious ring, but Holmes only asks to keep Irene's portrait—a souvenir of the case where Holmes' plan was thwarted by a woman's wit.

THE ADVENTURE OF THE RED-HEADED LEAGUE

"I know, my dear Watson, that you share my love of all that is bizarre and outside the conventions and humdrum routine of everyday life."
—Sherlock Holmes

WATSON DROPS IN ON HOLMES at Baker Street, to find him

with a man with bright red hair named Jabez Wilson. An owner of a pawnbroker's shop, Mr. Wilson has had a strange thing happen to him:

Just two months before, Mr. Wilson had responded to a call in the paper, summoning all red-headed men to apply for a vacancy at The Red-Headed League. The advertisement for the job had been brought to his attention by his new assistant, Vincent Spaulding, who said that he had heard the job paid well for nominal work, and that it would allow Wilson to make some extra money without taking him away too much from his responsibilities at the shop. To his pleasant surprise, Wilson won out over the throngs of other red-headed men who applied for the position. A man named Duncan Ross explained his duties. The only requirement was that he come to the building between the hours of 10 and 2 o'clock each day and transcribe the entire *Encyclopedia Britannica*. Mr. Wilson happily settled into his new job, until one morning he found the door locked, with a sign that read, "The Red-Headed League is dissolved." Wilson asked another tenant in the building if he knew what had happened, but curiously, he had never heard of The

Red-Headed League, or of Duncan Ross.

Now Mr. Wilson looks to Holmes for help. He is vexed at losing such a lucrative job, and he wants to know who could have played such an expensive prank. Holmes and Watson start by visiting Wilson's pawnshop, where they briefly encounter the young assistant Spaulding. Holmes notes that the knees of Spaulding's trousers are dirty. Holmes also ruminates on other things Wilson has told him about Spaulding: He has "come cheap" and is willing to work for half-wages. He likes photography, and is often going down in the pawnshop's cellar, where he has reportedly set up his darkroom.

Holmes then wanders around the block and notes the businesses: a tobacco shop, a newspaper stand, a restaurant . . . and a bank. Holmes seems satisfied with the day's investigations. He tells Watson to meet him back at Baker Street at 10 o'clock that night.

When Watson arrives he finds two more visitors: Inspector Peter Jones and Mr. Merryweather, the head of the bank. Holmes' plan is that they will thwart an impending bank robbery and finally apprehend a notorious criminal, John Clay. They all crouch down in the darkness of the bank vault, with their pistols ready. Soon the thieves make their appearance. Sure enough, it is John Clay (posing as Vincent Spaulding) and his accomplice (Duncan Ross), attempting to steal the 30,000 gold napoleons in the vault. Turns out the Red-Headed League was just a ruse: a way to get Jabez Wilson out of the shop while they dug their tunnel from the cellar to the bank's vault. It would have been a flawless crime—if it hadn't been for Sherlock Holmes!

THE MAN WITH THE TWISTED LIP

"It is, of course, a trifle, but there is nothing so important as trifles."
—Sherlock Holmes

I T'S LATE IN THE EVENING AT the Watson household, when there is an unexpected knock at the door. Mrs. Watson's old school chum has not seen her husband for two full days, but she knows just where he is: an opium den. Watson is recruited to retrieve the poor fellow from the place of iniquity, and he sets off for an unsavory part of the city: Upper Swandam Lane.

Watson finds the husband at the den, and just as he is about to leave he feels a tug from an old man with an opium pipe. It is Holmes in disguise! Holmes is there undercover, investigating a most baffling case:

the disappearance of one Neville
St. Clair.

Holmes supplies the details of
the case thus far to Watson: Mr. St.
Clair is a man of good reputation,
with a wife and two children. The
previous week, St. Clair went into
town for work as usual. The very
same day, his wife received a
telegram that summoned her to
Upper Swandam Lane to retrieve a
valuable package. While wandering

in this questionable neighborhood, she saw her husband from an upstairs window. Then just as suddenly, he disappeared. Flabbergasted, she rushed to the place where she spotted her husband, which was a room directly above the opium den. When she finally retrieved police constables to help her, they found only a "hideous cripple" and "professional beggar" in the room. His name is Hugh

Boone, and he has a memorably horrible face with an unspeakable scar and a twisted lip. Was he the last person to see St. Clair alive? St. Clair's clothes are found in the room, hidden behind the curtain. There is blood on the windowsill. And most suspiciously, St. Clair's coat is found in the Thames, with the pockets filled with pennies. Boone is arrested and taken in for questioning.

After Holmes relays these facts of the case to Watson, they both go to meet Mrs. St. Clair, who reports that her husband could not possibly be dead. She has received a letter from him, saying that "there is a huge error which may take some little time to rectify."

Holmes and Watson then pay a call to Boone in prison, where Holmes is armed with a water jug and a sponge. With one swipe of the sponge, the scar and twisted lip disappear, revealing that Boone is really St. Clair in disguise!

A contrite St. Clair explains: When he was in school, he got interested in the theatre, and in the art of using actor's makeup to transform himself into all sorts of characters. He eventually became a journalist. Going undercover for a story, he painted a terrible scar and a twisted lip on his face and posed as a beggar on a street corner. He drew on the sympathies of passers-by with his disfigured face, and to his pleasant surprise he made quite a bit of money that day, and the next. Begging as "Hugh Boone" was soon a profession he couldn't give up. He led a double life, renting a room above an opium den in order to change back to his respectable clothing before he returned to his family at the end of each day. He never dreamed he'd see his own wife in such a decrepit neighborhood—and certainly not accidentally locking eyes with her as he peered out the window! He panicked. Fearing discovery, he had hurriedly thrown his coat out the window into the river and accidentally cut himself on the ledge. With the police approaching, he stashed the rest of his clothes behind the curtain and quickly disguised himself as Hugh Boone. Ironically, he was arrested as his own murderer. He managed to send a letter, assuring his wife that he was alive, but he had been willing to go to the gallows to save the embarrassment of having to reveal his true profession. Now that he has confessed everything St. Clair is free to return to his respectable life, with the solemn promise that Hugh Boone will never again make another appearance on the streets of London.

THE ADVENTURE OF THE BLUE CARBUNCLE

"On the contrary, Watson, you see everything. You fail, however, to reason from what you see."
—Sherlock Holmes

EARLY ONE CHRISTMAS morning, a man named Peterson passes a man on the street carrying a fat goose over his shoulder. Suddenly a band of thugs attacks the man and Peterson rushes in to help. The man runs off, leaving his hat and his Christmas goose behind. Knowing that Holmes likes to solve small problems, Peterson brings the goose and the hat to Baker Street to see if Holmes can identify the man and return his hat. As for the goose, it's prudently decided that it should be cooked and enjoyed by Peterson and his family that day.

But Peterson soon returns with the most incredible news: A precious gem has been found inside the goose's carcass! Holmes guesses that it must be the Countess of Morcar's blue carbuncle, which has recently been stolen and carries a rich reward for its return. Recalling what he has read in the papers, Holmes says that a plumber named

John Homer has been indicted for stealing the carbuncle from the Countess' room at the Hotel Cosmopolitan.

Using his powers of deduction, Holmes determines that the owner of the lost hat is one Henry Baker, who soon comes to retrieve his lost items. He is pleased when Holmes tells him that another bird has been bought for him to take home to his family, thus proving his innocence.

He must not know about the blue carbuncle.

Holmes and Watson then go to investigate where the Blue Carbuncle goose had been sold. Their search leads to a shopkeeper in Covent Garden, where they find another man desperately inquiring about the goose. The man is James Ryder, head attendant of the Hotel Cosmopolitan. Knowing that he has been cornered, Ryder confesses everything to Holmes. It was really Ryder—in cahoots with the Countess' maid—who had stolen the gem, and framed Homer. Ryder wanted to find a safe place to hide the carbuncle, so he went to visit his sister, who raises geese and sells them to the local markets. He quickly thrust the stone down a goose's throat, with the intention that he would ask his sister for that particular goose to take home for his Christmas dinner.

But the goose wandered back to its gaggle, and in his confusion Ryder had taken home the wrong bird.

At the end of this confession, Ryder begs Holmes for mercy. He has never committed a crime before. He has been overtaken with greed, and is truly sorry. Holmes lets him go, saying that it's the "season of forgiveness" and feels confident that the case against Homer will soon be dropped.

THE ADVENTURE OF THE SPECKLED BAND

"Violence does, in truth, recoil upon the violent, and the schemer falls into the pit which he digs for another."
— Sherlock Holmes

A YOUNG LADY VISITS THE flat at Baker Street, looking weary and haggard, her hair prematurely white. Her name is Helen Stoner, and she lives with her stepfather, Dr. Grimesby Roylott, on his crumbling estate of Stoke Moran. She explains to Holmes and Watson what has led to her distress:

Helen's mother, a woman of considerable fortune, had died eight years before, and in her will she made provisions for Helen and her twin sister, Julia. Their stepfather was to manage their money until they marry. After his wife's death, Dr. Roylott's behavior became erratic and bizarre: He displayed frequent bursts of violent temper, and kept a strange menagerie. He had a fondness for animals from exotic parts of the world and allowed a cheetah and baboon to freely wander the estate. Helen and Julia did their best to live normally under such conditions.

Helen goes on to report it has been two years since her sister's untimely demise. Julia was engaged to be married, and as her wedding date approached, Julia remarked to Helen that she had been hearing a low, clear whistle in the middle of the night. They both dismissed it, but one night Helen awoke to the terrified shriek of her twin. She rushed to Julia's room, to find her convulsing and writhing in pain. Her last words were, "Oh My God! Helen! It was the band, the speckled band!"

Helen confirms that Julia's bedroom door had been locked from the inside. The chimney had been blocked. And there were no marks of violence upon her. The only conclusion, in Helen's estimation, was that her sister had died of shock. But she can't determine what could have frightened Julia to death.

Now, two years later, Helen

reports that she is about to be married, and that she has begun to hear that same nocturnal whistle. What's more, due to household repairs, she has moved her bedroom and is now sleeping in the same place where her sister died. She is beside herself with fear, and asks Holmes to come to the estate to investigate.

Almost immediately after Helen's departure, Dr. Roylott

bursts into the drawing room. He has followed his stepdaughter, and warns them not to meddle in his affairs.

Undeterred, Holmes does a little research and discovers that, once Helen marries, Dr. Roylott will be left without a cent. Holmes and Watson then go to the estate and inspect Helen's bedroom. There is a bell-pull that dangles over Helen's pillow, which is attached to a ventilator that connects to Dr. Roylott's bedroom. In Dr. Roylott's chambers they find a saucer of milk, a dog leash tied in a loop, and a large iron safe. Holmes examines these clues and knows he must carry out a daring mission to prevent another murder.

That night, Holmes and Watson keep vigil in Helen's bedroom. They see a light coming from the ventilator. Holmes lights a match and strikes with his cane at the bell-pull. They hear the low whistle, then a most blood-curdling scream from Dr. Roylott's bedroom. They find Dr. Roylott dead, with a strange yellow band around his brow. Holmes whispers, "The band, the speckled band!" It's a swamp adder, the deadliest snake in India. Holmes takes the dog-whip and coaxes the horrid snake back into the iron safe.

Holmes explains: The swamp adder provided the perfect method for Roylott to carry out his dastardly scheme, to kill his step-daughters before they married. The adder's fangs leave tiny marks that are not detected and they have an untraceable form of venom. Roylott coaxed the snake through the ventilator and down the bell-pull every night, knowing that sooner or later the snake would bite its victim. The saucer of milk and the dog leash were used to train the snake to return to Roylott upon hearing his low whistle. But this last time, Holmes had roused the snake's temper with the swipes of his cane, causing it to attack its master. Holmes knows that he is somewhat responsible for Roylott's death, but he admits that it will not weigh very heavily upon his conscience.

THE ADVENTURE OF THE COPPER BEECHES

"The lowest and vilest alleys
in London do not present a more
dreadful record of sin than does the
smiling and beautiful countryside."
—Sherlock Holmes

A YOUNG WOMAN NAMED
Violet Hunter seeks
Holmes' counsel: Should

she accept a governess position, one that sounds too good to be true? A seemingly affable fellow named Jephro Rucastle has offered her a very handsome salary to take care of his six-year-old son, in an isolated but "charmingly rural" place called the Copper Beeches. But there are a few strange requirements: Would she mind terribly wearing a certain dress at certain times of the day? And he really must insist that she cut her hair short. Miss Hunter is uneasy about agreeing to such requests, but the money is too good to turn down. She would feel better about accepting the employment if she could rely on Holmes' assistance if she finds herself in danger. Holmes is intrigued and assures her that she need only beckon him with a telegram if she is in jeopardy.

That telegram comes just two

weeks later. Holmes and Watson catch the next train to the nearest town of Winchester, where they meet Miss Hunter. Though visibly shaken, she goes on to calmly and competently report her bizarre experiences since her arrival at Copper Beeches:

First, Miss Hunter paints a precise picture of all the members of the household: Along with the agreeable Mr. Rucastle is his much younger wife, who is pale, anxious, and chronically sad. Their little boy Edward vacillates between fits of temper and quiet gloom. Mr. Rucastle had been a widower before marrying his second wife, and he has a twenty-year-old daughter named Alice from his first marriage, and she is reportedly living in Philadelphia. The only servants are Toller, who appears to be drunk most of the time, and his sour-faced and silent wife. There is one last frightening member of the estate: Mr. Rucastle's ferocious mastiff, who is kept under lock and key during the day. At night the beast is let loose on the grounds to patrol for trespassers. Rucastle admits that the dog is so wild he can't tame him—only Toller is able to handle the creature.

Within a few days of arriving, Miss Hunter says, she was asked to change into a bright blue dress and sit with her back to the window of the drawing room. There Mr. Rucastle told her amusing stories, which made her laugh heartily. A few days later, she was asked to wear the dress again, sit in the same place, and Mr. Rucastle told more tales that inspired her glee. Both times she felt that there was someone watching her. Unable to quell her curiosity, upon her next "performance" she hid a piece of mirror into her handkerchief and confirmed there was indeed a man observing her from outside.

Miss Hunter continues her strange tale. Sentimental about losing her lovely hair for the job, Miss Hunter packed the coil of her shorn hair at the bottom of her trunk, and brought it with her to Copper Beeches. As she settled into her new bedroom, she came across a locked drawer to the dresser. She retrieved the keys and opened the drawer to find . . . what looked to be the coil of her own hair! The coil was almost identical to her own, with the same shade, texture, and length. What could be the explanation?

The last event was the most menacing of all, and what inspired Miss Hunter to send for Holmes' help. She had noticed a shuttered wing of the house. Mr. Rucastle explained that he had built a dark room there to support his photography hobby, but his usual merry tone turned threatening, making it clear that she was not to explore that section of the house. Overwhelmed by curiosity, she ventured into the forbidden territory, where she discovered a room with a padlocked door and noticed a shadow pass underneath. She then ran straight into Mr. Rucastle, who warned her that he would throw her to the dog if he ever found her there again.

Upon concluding this extraordinary tale, Miss Hunter looks to Holmes for a plan. The Rucastles are expected to be out that night, so the coast should be clear for Holmes and Watson to investigate. Once there, they burst open the padlocked room, where they find an empty cell. Mr. Rucastle suddenly appears, and Holmes demands of him, "Where's your daughter?" The villain runs to let the mastiff loose. Toller warns that the dog "has not been fed for two days! Quick or it'll be too late!" A blood-curdling cry tells them that it is indeed too late: The dog has sunk his teeth into Rucastle's neck. Watson shoots the dog, saving Rucastle's life.

All is eventually explained by Mrs. Toller: Mr. Rucastle's daughter Alice had fallen in love. Mr. Rucastle knew that he couldn't control Alice's handsome inheritance if she married, so he took extreme measures to ward off her suitor, Mr. Fowler. Alice fell ill with brain fever, which meant her hair had to be cut off. She eventually recovered, but by then her father had already grown accustomed to her being confined to her room. So he kept his daughter prisoner, while he hired someone who bore a striking resemblance to her, down to the exact shade of hair. The displays of conviviality with Miss Hunter in the drawing room were staged to show Mr. Fowler that his sweetheart was happy without him. But the ruse didn't work. Mrs. Toller acted as accomplice to Mr. Fowler, helping him to lead Alice out of her cell that very evening.

Justice is served: Rucastle is left

permanently disfigured from his injury. Alice and Fowler elope, and Miss Hunter, Watson reports, goes on to become a school head-mistress. Watson intimates that Holmes had admired Miss Hunter's bravery and her knack for precise observation, but any hint of an attachment was coolly dismissed after the case was solved.

SILVER BLAZE

Colonel Ross: *"Is there any point to which you would wish to draw my attention?"*

Holmes: *"To the curious incident of the dog in the nighttime."*

Ross: *"The dog did nothing in the nighttime."*

Holmes: *"That was the curious incident."*

H OLMES AND WATSON GO to Dartmoor to investigate a high-profile case. A champion horse, Silver Blaze, has gone missing, and his trainer, John Straker, has been found murdered. Holmes has been summoned by the horse's owner, Colonel Ross, to investigate. Holmes reviews the details of the case as they ride the train:

On the night in question, Silver Blaze was settled in his stable, with a stable-boy named Hunter watching over him. John Straker and his wife live nearby, and their maid took Hunter's dinner out to him—a curried mutton, to be precise. On her way across the moor, the maid encountered a stranger, who followed her to the stable, where he asked for a tip for the upcoming Wessex Cup. The boy sicced his dog on him, and the stranger ran away. The boy ate his dinner and fell asleep, while two other lads slept in the loft above him.

Mrs. Straker reported that her husband awakened in the middle of that night and went out to check on the horse. His body was found on the moor the next morning, his head having suffered a fierce blow from a heavy object. In one of the victim's hands was a small, delicate knife, while the other clutched a cravat—identified as belonging to the stranger, now revealed to be one Fitzroy Simpson. Hunter's curry had been drugged—and the horse was nowhere to be found. So far, everything about the case points to Simpson, but the police only have circumstantial evidence.

Once in Dartmoor, Holmes asks for an inventory of the victim's pockets. Of interest is a bill from a lady's dress shop for a very expensive frock. After Holmes questions Mrs. Straker, it's clear she does not own the purchased dress. They then visit the cantankerous Silas Brown, the keeper of a competing champion horse. Holmes whispers in Brown's ear, and his face falls. Holmes knows that he is hiding Silver Blaze. Watson observes Brown and Holmes working out a deal, but Holmes does not offer further explanation. He has found Silver Blaze's abductor, but he has more work to do to pinpoint Straker's killer.

Through his queries, Holmes zeroes in on a very important clue: The "curious incident of the dog in the night-time" is that the dog did not bark.

A few days later, everyone attends the Wessex Cup, where a mysterious horse wins the race.

The winner turns out to be Silver Blaze, whose markings have been covered with heavy soot to disguise him. Then Holmes states that he has found Straker's killer. It's . . . . Silver Blaze! Holmes provides the explanation:

It couldn't have been the stranger Simpson who drugged the boy's curry with powdered opium. The drug has a distinctive taste, which can only be disguised with something like curry. Someone inside the Straker household must have planned to serve curry that evening, in order to fit into a larger scheme. That person was John Straker: He drugged the boy so that he could sneak the horse out of its stable, out on the moor. Why didn't the dog bark and wake up the other lads sleeping in the loft? Because the dog knew Straker well, and didn't see him as a threat.

Straker took Silver Blaze to a secluded spot, intending to nick the horse's tendon, hence the small knife in his hand. Along the way, he picked up a dropped cravat on the path, thinking he might need it to restrain the horse's leg. His motive for hobbling his own horse? He needed money, so his plan was to bet heavily against Silver Blaze, then injure him to prevent him from winning. The dress bill in his pocket revealed the cause of his money troubles: He had a mistress with expensive tastes.

Alas, Straker didn't count on Silver Blaze's fear and fury. The horse rose up and struck Straker on the forehead with his horse-shoed hoof, killing him instantly. The horse then wandered the moor, where it was abducted by Silas Brown, who wanted to keep the horse hidden until after the big race. Holmes shows mercy, and does not report Brown to the police. Holmes reasons that Brown made an impulsive error in judgment in hiding the horse, but it was Straker who had the pre-meditated, elaborate scheme. Justice has inadvertently been carried out—not by man, but by beast.

THE ADVENTURE OF THE MUSGRAVE RITUAL

"You can imagine, Watson, with what eagerness I listened to this extraordinary sequence of events, and endeavored to piece them together, and to devise some common thread upon which they might all hang."

—Sherlock Holmes

GOING THROUGH MEMEN-toes, Holmes is reminded of a case that happened many years before. He tells Watson about his old school acquaintance Reginald Musgrave, who had consulted Holmes on a most puzzling matter:

Musgrave had inherited his father's estate, which required many servants and much upkeep.

One of the most trusted servants was Brunton the butler. Efficient in almost every way, his only "fault" perhaps was that he was a bit of a Don Juan. He had just jilted the second housemaid, Rachel Howells, in favor of another girl.

One night, Musgrave couldn't sleep and he wandered into the library, where he found Brunton pouring over a map, as well as a slip of paper that he had taken from the bureau. Musgrave became indignant, demanding to know what Brunton had stolen from the family documents. To his surprise, the paper contained nothing of any consequence, but he still found it necessary to dismiss Brunton for betraying the family's trust. The chastened butler begged to be given a week to prepare for his dismissal. Two days later, he vanished. Curiously, he left all his clothes, watch, and money in his room. Upon the news of his disappearance, Rachel became hysterical, and she went missing as well. They followed her footsteps to a lake, where it was assumed that she became demented in her grief and committed suicide. They had the lake dragged to search for the body, but they found only a linen bag filled with pieces of metal and glass. The police were baffled, so

Musgrave found it necessary to visit his old school chum to help solve the mystery: What could have become of the butler and his former lover?

Holmes inquired about the contents of the piece of paper that Brunton had taken from the drawer. Musgrave said it was only a nonsensical series of questions-and-answers, something that had been passed down for generations of

Musgraves. Holmes eventually deduced that this "Musgrave Ritual" was actually cryptic directions for finding a treasure. Crafty enough to uncrack the ritual's codes, Brunton had been hot on the trail of finding the treasure when he had been caught in the library.

Holmes then used the "ritual" to locate the treasure site, where he found Brunton dead, trapped and suffocated under a heavy slab.

Holmes logically guessed how Brunton could have met with such a cruel fate: He reasoned that Brunton had no choice but to enlist Rachel's help, knowing that it would take two people to lift the heavy stone and get to the treasure. They lifted the slab up and Brunton must have gone down the hole in pursuit of the riches. He lifted a linen bag up to her, while she, in a fit of passion over having been spurned, sent the stone crashing down upon Brunton, burying him alive. This explained her strange behavior after Brunton's disappearance. She must have thrown the bag into the lake to remove any trace of her crime, then somehow escaped out of England.

The metal and glass in the bag turned out to be the coins and the ring of King Charles the First. After the sovereign's overthrow more than two hundred years before, the long line of Musgrave royalists had constructed the "ritual" to point toward the family's secret possessions.

Upon recounting this tale, Holmes reflects with satisfaction on his role in uncovering these historic relics.

THE FINAL PROBLEM

*"He is the Napoleon
of Crime, Watson."*
—Sherlock Holmes

I T IS WITH A HEAVY HEART THAT I take up my pen," Watson writes as he reports on his last account of his friend's remarkable gifts as a sleuth.

Ten years have passed since they first lived together on Baker Street, and Watson admits he has lost touch with his old friend. Watson has been busy with his medical practice and his domestic life, but he has read in the paper of Holmes' involvement in a case with the French government.

Watson is surprised, then, when Holmes makes a sudden appearance at his clinic. Holmes immediately draws the shutters and nervously peeks outside. He looks pale and drawn, like he has lost much sleep over the course of months. Indeed, Holmes confirms that he is gravely troubled.

Through his investigations, Holmes has discovered a brilliant but dangerous man—Professor Moriarty. He is a criminal genius and mastermind of many of the evil schemes that have happened not just in London, but also abroad—everything from forgeries, to burglaries, and to murders. His agents can be found everywhere, ready to carry out his machinations. Holmes has been working tirelessly to thwart some of Moriarty's diabolical plans, but admits he has met his intellectual match. He has hopes that he is near catching Moriarty and that the police will have what they need to arrest him, but so far his rival has managed to stay one step ahead.

That very morning, Holmes reports, he found himself face-to-face with his arch-foe. Making a surprise visit to Baker Street, Moriarty warned him to cease his investigations, and when Holmes refused, the professor assured him he has sealed his "inevitable destruction." Moriarty is a man who makes good on his promises:

Since the morning Holmes has narrowly escaped a falling brick and a random attack on the street—both incidents carried out by Moriarty's ubiquitous helpers.

Holmes plans to flee to the Continent, and asks Watson to join him. An elaborate plan is hatched which involves Holmes once again deceiving Watson with one of his disguises (this time as an Italian priest). The old friends make their way to Switzerland, where they enjoy the Alpine villages, eventually coming to the village of Meiringen. There they are warned about going too near Reichenbach Falls, as it's a dangerous chasm, with jagged rocks and a "long sweep of green water roaring forever down."

They set out on a hike toward Reichenbach Falls, but Watson is summoned back to the hotel to attend to a guest who has suddenly taken ill. He has qualms about leaving Holmes, but it sounds like such an emergency and he cannot in good conscience ignore the call. He leaves Holmes, "with his back against a rock and his arms folded, gazing down at the rush of waters."

Once back at the hotel, Watson realizes he's been duped. There is no sick guest. He immediately runs back to where he left Holmes.

There is only a letter, folded and left under a boulder. It's from Holmes, informing Watson that he has gone to meet Moriarty, for "the final discussion of those questions that lie between us." He trusts that he will be able to "free society from any further effects of his presence," but hints that it may be at the cost of his own life.

Watson can only surmise the worst: The two men must have had a face-off at the edge of the falls, and it must have ended with both of them toppling into the chasm of Reichenbach, with no chance of finding either of the bodies.

But can Watson be certain Holmes is dead?

THE HOUND OF THE BASKERVILLES

"Mr. Holmes, they were the footprints of a gigantic hound!"
—Dr. Mortimer

A COUNTRY SURGEON NAMED Dr. James Mortimer consults with Holmes, saying he has a matter that weighs upon his conscience. A recent event may have ties to an old legend:

Back in 1782, Hugo Baskerville kidnapped a local girl and brought her to his manor, intending to compromise her honor. While he got drunk with his squires, the girl escaped and ran across the moor. Enraged, Hugo released his dogs in chase of the poor maiden. Hugo and his party followed on the hunt. The girl died of exhaustion and fear. But Hugo met with a much crueler fate: A ferocious black hound, larger than any mortal had ever seen, had plucked at his throat with his huge jaws. According to legend, the Hound of the Baskervilles has haunted the family ever since.

Now Hugo's descendant, Sir Charles Baskerville, has just been found dead. Charles had been a generous benefactor to his community, and his death interrupts many of his intended good deeds. Knowing of his family's curse, he was superstitious about venturing out on the moor after dark, yet he still took nightly walks on his own grounds. He died of cardiac arrest, his face contorted with fear. Dr. Mortimer had been summoned the night of Charles' death, and he saw something he didn't report at the inquest: The footprints of a gigantic hound were found near the body. As a man of science, he doesn't want to believe in the Curse of the Baskervilles, but he suspects something supernatural may be responsible for Sir Charles' death.

Now Baskerville Hall passes on to Charles' nephew, Sir Henry Baskerville, who has come in from Canada to claim the estate. Sir Henry has received an anonymous letter, warning him to stay away.

His boots have mysteriously disappeared from his London hotel, and it seems he is being followed. Holmes tells Henry that he must not go to Baskerville Hall without taking Watson along for protection. But Holmes will stay in London, as he has pressing business that will keep him in the city.

Sir Henry and Watson travel to the foggy, foreboding landscape of Devon, where they find Baskerville

Hall to be gloomy and off-putting.
The creepiness of the atmosphere
is heightened by the news that
there is an escaped murderer
named Selden on the loose. They
meet the servants, Barrymore and
his wife; as well as the neighbors,
Jack Stapleton and his sister Beryl.
Stapleton is a naturalist, a mild-
looking man who likes to wander
the moor to collect specimens for
his botany studies. Where Staple-

ton is gray and colorless, Miss Stapleton is a striking, dark beauty. There is another neighbor, an elderly man named Mr. Frankland, who delights in knowing everyone's business.

When Miss Stapleton meets Watson, she assumes he is Sir Henry, and desperately warns him to leave the estate. When she realizes her mistake she tries to make nothing of it, and nervously looks to her brother. As the days pass, Watson notes a growing attachment between Miss Stapleton and Sir Henry. The potential lovers have a rendezvous on the moor, where Stapleton angrily confronts them. Stapleton later apologizes for his outburst.

Meanwhile, it's revealed that Mrs. Barrymore is the elder sister of the convict Selden. She and her husband have been harboring the fugitive, taking food out to him on the moor. They beg Watson and Sir Henry not to tell the authorities, but to allow them to arrange his passage abroad, where he will no longer be a menace to English society. In gratitude for their silence, Barrymore gives them an interesting tidbit regarding Sir Charles' death: On the night he died, he was waiting for a woman. The lady's initials are "L.L." and they had planned to meet at 10 o'clock by the gate.

The woman turns out to be Laura Lyons, Frankland's daughter. She had made an imprudent marriage, and was abandoned by her husband and disowned by her father. Upon interrogation, Laura admits that she had written to Sir Charles, asking for his help with her divorce expenses. As a generous benefactor, he had been willing to assist with cases such as hers, and she thought she might better persuade him if she told of her plight in person. But on the night in question she decided not to meet him after all.

The busybody Frankland proudly tells Watson that he knows where Selden is hiding—he has spotted a boy taking out food on the moor. Watson visits the primitive hut where someone has been taking shelter. It is not Selden... but Sherlock Holmes! He has not been in London all this time, but secretly camping on the moor. He found it necessary to deceive Watson so that he could get an outsider's view on all that is happening around Baskerville Hall. He has made some crucial discoveries: Beryl Stapleton is not Jack Stapleton's sister—but rather his wife! Jack Stapleton is their villain, a "man with a smiling face but a murderous heart." Holmes will tell Watson the particulars later. But for now, they need to entrap him—just like a butterfly in Stapleton's nets.

They hear a scream and run to find a man fallen on the rocks. The dead man is Selden, wearing Sir Henry's tweeds. Mrs. Barrymore had given her brother the clothes to wear for his escape. Since Stapleton has trained the dog to attack on Sir

Henry's scent, the purloined clothes have sealed his doom. The terrified Selden must have run off a cliff, with the hound close at his heels.

Holmes tells Sir Henry that he must follow his plan to the letter, as his life depends upon it. He is to accept the Stapleton's invitation to dinner that night. Then he is to say he will walk home across the moor. Holmes sends for Scotland Yard's Inspector Lestrade, who will help with the ambush.

The bait has been set: Sir Henry walks on the moor, the thick fog encroaching. Suddenly, the horrible, savage creature appears and chases him. Holmes, Watson, and Lestrade come to his rescue, shooting the dog dead. They run to Stapleton's house, where they find Beryl bound and gagged. Stapleton has made his getaway . . . yet Holmes concludes he has met his end in the dreadful Grimpen Mire, a bog with quicksand that can swallow up any creature, leaving no trace.

Holmes explains everything: The man calling himself Stapleton was really a Baskerville, the son of Sir Charles' brother, who had long ago decamped for South America. Stapleton had married a Costa Rican beauty, Beryl, and they both came to England. He found it a better decoy if his wife posed as his sister.

Only two persons separated Stapleton from the Baskerville estate: Sir Charles and Sir Henry. Knowing the legend of the Curse of the Baskervilles, Stapleton used it to his advantage. He acquired a savage dog, and painted it black with phosphorous to make it look even more terrifying. He kept the beast on an island in the middle of the Grimpen Mire, a place he knew few men could penetrate.

He enlisted the unsuspecting Laura Lyons to help with his plan. Posing as a single man, he made overtures of love to her. He then encouraged her to write to Sir Charles to help with her divorce, and arrange a secret meeting. At the appointed time, he brought the hound to the gate, and weak-hearted Charles had died of fright. Then Stapleton came to London and stole Sir Henry's boots, which would help him train the dog to attack on Henry's scent.

At first, Stapleton was jealous when he noticed Sir Henry falling in love with his "sister." But he realized that this could also work to his advantage. The growing attachment assured that Sir Henry would be making many trips across the moor to visit Beryl, and there would be ample opportunity for the dog to attack its intended victim. But on that frighteningly foggy night, Beryl had turned on her husband, perhaps wanting to save her suitor. Stapleton tied her up until his carefully crafted scheme could be completed.

Alas, he had not planned on Holmes making an appearance and foiling his plan.

SHERLOCK HOLMES BIBLIOGRAPHY

THE NOVELS

A Study in Scarlet

The Sign of Four

The Hound of the Baskervilles

The Valley of Fear

THE SHORT STORIES

The Adventures of Sherlock Holmes, comprised of:

"A Scandal in Bohemia"

"The Adventure of the Red-Headed League"

"The Adventure of the Musgrave Ritual"

"The Adventure of the Reigate Squire"

"The Adventure of the Crooked Man"

"The Adventure of the Resident Patient"

"The Adventure of the Greek Interpreter"

"The Adventure of the Naval Treaty"

"The Final Problem"

The Return of Sherlock Holmes, comprised of:

"The Adventure of the Empty House"

"The Adventure of the Norwood Builder"

"The Adventure of the Dancing Men"

"The Adventure of the Solitary Cyclist"

"The Adventure of the Priory School"

"The Adventure of Black Peter"

"The Adventure of Charles Augustus Milverton"

"The Adventure of the Six Napoleons"

The Case-Book of Sherlock Holmes, comprised of:

"The Adventure of the Mazarin Stone"

"The Problem of Thor Bridge"

"The Adventure of the Creeping Man"

"The Adventure of the Sussex Vampire"

"The Adventure of the Three Garridebs"

"The Adventure of the Illustrious Client"

"The Adventure of the Three Gables"

"The Adventure of the Blanched Soldier"

"The Adventure of the Lion's Mane"

"The Adventure of the Retired Colourman"

"The Adventure of the Veiled Lodger"

"The Adventure of Shoscombe Old Place"

ILLUSTRATION CREDITS

This book has been bound using
handcraft methods and
Smyth-sewn to ensure durability.

Designed by Amanda Richmond.

Written by Jennifer Kasius.

Edited by Cindy De La Hoz.

The text was set in Chronicle.